Read with Me:

Here are some fun activities to prepare your child for reading this book. Take just a few minutes to help your child master new words and reading skills.

Rhyming: Say a word and ask your child to say one that has the same ending sound. For example, you say "day," and your child might say "play."

cat   tail   see   hug

Sight words: Say each of these words aloud, and help your child find the word in this book. Let your child color in a star beside each word he or she reads.

☆ thinking   ☆ someone   ☆ computers   ☆ created

To, With and By: This technique introduces words into your child's ears first. Then it helps your child to match the words he or she hears to the print on the page.

To: Read the entire story out loud *to* your child. Run your finger under the words as you say them at a normal speed.

With: Read the same story two times *with* your child. Don't slow down, and make sure your child is looking at the words while you read.

By: Let your child read the story *by* himself or herself. Help fix any mistakes.

Have your child read this story for the next several days until it sounds great and is practically memorized.

Dedicated to
my husband, David.

Faith Kids® is an imprint of
Cook Communications Ministries, Colorado Springs, CO 80918
Cook Communications, Paris, Ontario
Kingsway Communications, Eastbourne, England

GUESS WHO LOVES ME
©2001 by Cook Communications Ministries

First printing, 2001
Printed in Canada

1 2 3 4 5 6 7 8 9 10   Printing/Year 05 04 03 02 01

Edited by: Susan Martins Miller
Cover and Interior Design: Scott Johnson
Illustrated by: Steven Brite

ISBN: 0-7814-3549-8

GOD PRINTS

Guess Who Loves Me?

Written by Peggy Wilber

Illustrations by Steven Brite

Equipping Kids for Life!
faithkids.com

"OK, Herbie, it's my turn to play," said Pris.
"I am thinking of someone who loves me."

"Does he have a tail?
Does he have claws?
And does he purr?"
asked Herbie.

"Is it Slink, the cat?" he asked.

"I'm not thinking of Slink, the cat, but he does love me," said Pris.

"Does he have wings
and a beak?

Does he like to eat bugs
and have a red tie?"
asked Herbie.

"Is he Swoop, the blue jay?"
asked Herbie.

"I'm not thinking of Swoop," said Pris. "But he loves me when I feed him seeds."

Herbie asked, "Does he have a tail and four paws?

Does he bark?"

"Is he Wally, the sheepdog?" asked Herbie.
"No, it's not Wally, but he loves to get a treat," said Pris.
"Do you want a treat too, Digby?"

"Does he wear glasses and have freckles?"

"Does he like computers?
Is it PJ, your brother?" asked Herbie.

"PJ loves me even when I bug him, but it's not my brother," said Pris.

"Is he big?
Does he have brown hair?
Is it my cousin, Hammer?"
asked Herbie.

"Hammer loves me even when he doesn't show it, but I'm not thinking of Hammer," said Pris.

"Does she have wings

and a tail that lights up
at night?" asked Herbie.

"Does Twinkles, the firefly, love you?" asked Herbie.

"No, it's not Twinkles," said Pris.

"I'm thinking of someone
who really loves me,"
she said.
Herbie asked, "Does
she take care of you
and give lots of hugs?

Does she put you to bed
every night?
Are you thinking of your
mother?" asked Herbie.

"My mother really loves me, but I am thinking of someone else," said Pris.

"I am thinking of someone
who created me
and who watches over me
day and night."

"I know who it is," said Herbie.
"It's God! God loves you."

"You are right," said Pris.
"Good night, Herbie.
God loves you too!"

Godprint: Preciousness

Did you know God made you? And he loves you just for you. No one else is just like you. You're precious, just like Pris!

Psalm 121:7-8
The LORD will keep you from every kind of harm. He will watch over your life. The LORD will watch over your life no matter where you go, both now and forever.